B.B.- For Stacey, Lea, Brett, and all the EMTs and Paramedics I have worked with over 25 years.

M.A.-For Paul and all the lives he's saved.

On a very nice day,
I was out for a ride,
When I saw a white van,
With a star on the side.

I thought to myself,
"What a cool place to go.
They must have great stories,
And neat things to show!"

I opened the back doors,
And felt really "smooth",
They turned on the siren,
And my feet started to move!

But the man in the white shirt said…

"Please don't dance... in my ambulance!"

This is not for fun!
We help people who are hurt.
But you may ride along,
But be ready, and alert!

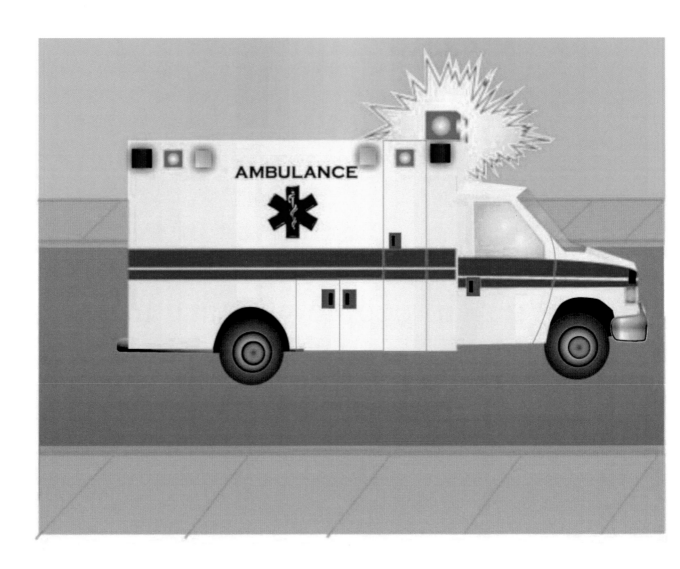

We sped to the scene,
Our red lights were a 'gleaming.
The cars all moved over
When the siren was screaming.

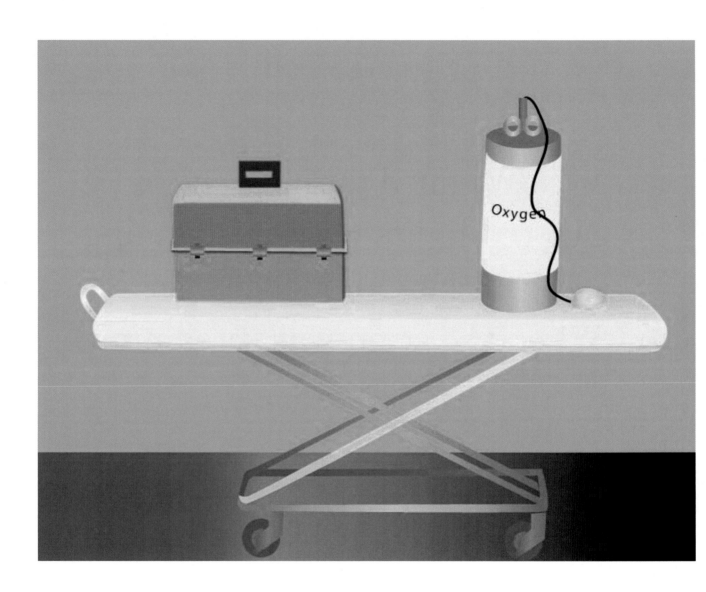

The stretcher,
The first aid box too,
Grab the oxygen tank,
In case his face is blue.

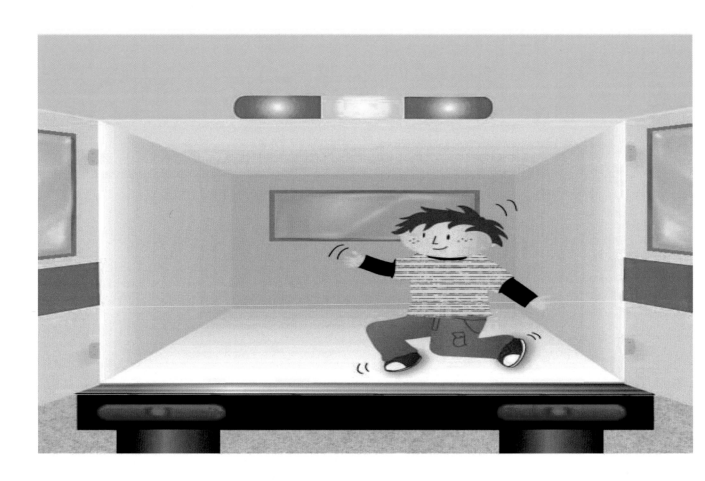

A real-life emergency call!
I thought it was so neat!
So I jumped in the back,
And started moving my feet!

But the E.M.T. in the white shirt said....

"Please don't dance... in my ambulance!"

This man needs our help.
There is work to be done.
This is _serious_.
No time for fun!

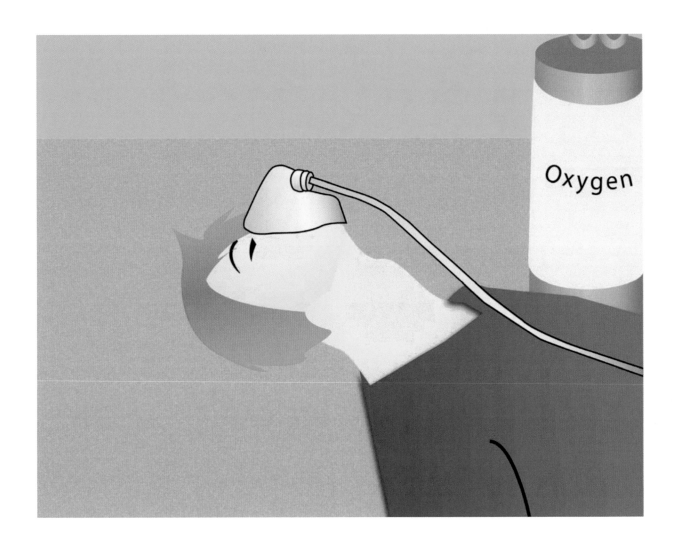

We put an oxygen mask on his face,
And some medicine in his arm,
His breathing got better,
It worked like a charm!

We took him to the hospital,
And in a very short while,
The man felt much better,
And said "Thanks!" with a smile.

We helped save a life.
We made quite a crew!
Our work is done for the day,
So here's what we'll do...

So the man in the white shirt said...

NOW we can dance…
in my ambulance!

THE END

About the author and illustrator

Barry Bachenheimer is a teacher and administrator in New Jersey. He has been involved in Emergency Medical Services for over 25 years.

Mea Amacher is an art teacher in New Jersey. Her husband is a New Jersey certified paramedic.